Anneena came round to play.
"Let's go out," said Biff. "Let's
go down to the playground."

1

They got to the playground, but they found it was locked up.

The roundabout was broken.
The playhouse was broken. The swings
had tape round them.

They saw a man from the council.
"It was not safe," said the man.
"So now it has been shut down."

"Will they fix it?" asked Mum.
"No," said the man. "It would cost
ten thousand pounds."

They met Wilf and Wilma.
"It's bad news," said Biff. "The playground
has been shut down."

"It will cost thousands to fix it," said Anneena. "Could we get the money?"

"We need ten thousand pounds . . .

. . . to get a new playground . . .

. . . pass it round . . .

. . . shout about it!"

The mums and dads met at Anneena's house.

"Let's have a Summer Fair," said Wilma's mum. "That will make money."

Anneena's dad went round the town.
He had a megaphone.

"Come to the Summer Fair," he shouted. "We need money for the playground."

A big crowd came to the Summer Fair.

There were lots of stalls. The scouts had a stall and so did the brownies.

There was a bouncy castle to bounce on.

There was a clown in baggy trousers.
He had a flower that spouted
out water.

Anneena's dad was the announcer. "Look up at the sky," he shouted to the crowd.

Sky divers came out of the clouds
and landed on the ground.
"I would love to do that," said Wilf.

"We raised about ten thousand pounds," said Dad.

"So now we can get a new playground," said Anneena.

The children loved the new playground.

But Floppy had to stay outside.
Dogs were not allowed.

"How about a playground for dogs?"
said Kipper.